A Gift To You From

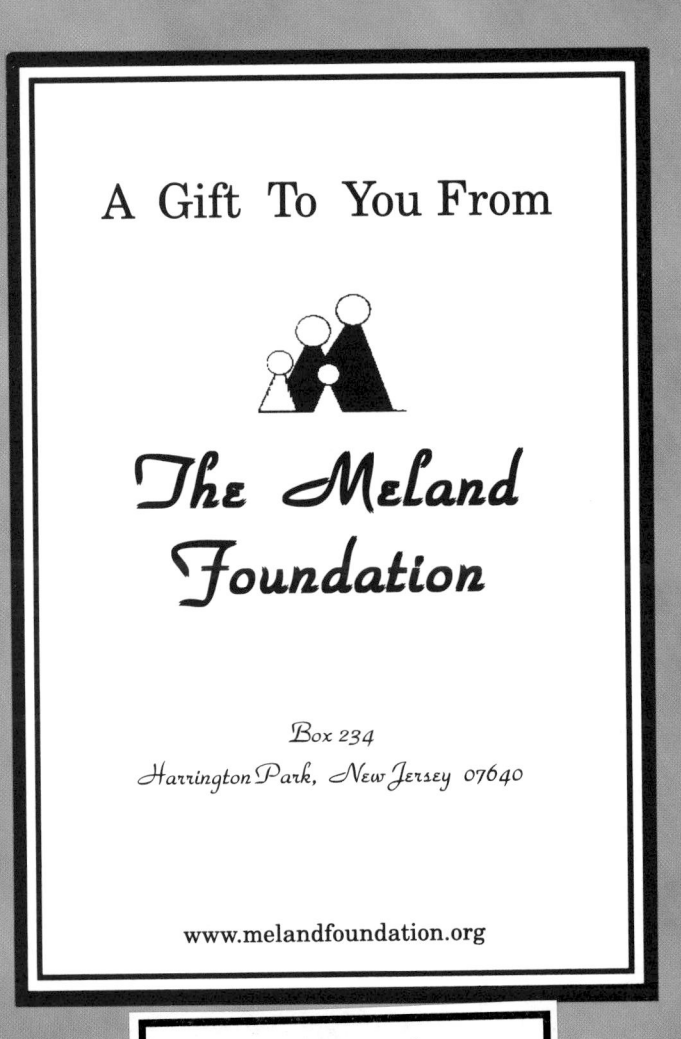

*The Meland*
*Foundation*

*Box 234*
*Harrington Park, New Jersey 07640*

www.melandfoundation.org

*In Honor of*
*Ching-Hon Pui, MD*

# Hang On, Hester!

## A Story of Courage and the Power of Example

## by Wende and Harry Devlin

Published by DCN Publishing Co.

Inquiries should be adressed to

DCN Publishing Co.
Box 234
Harrington Park, New Jersey 07640

Revised Edition
1 2 3 4 5 6 7 8 9 10

Library of Congress Catalog Card Number 98-74750
Devlin, Wende
Hang On, Hester!

Our appreciation to Imaging Dynamics for serving as a consultant in
graphics and to Ed Miller for assisting with the cover and book design

Printed by
Nicholstone

in the USA

SUMMARY
Hester courageously hangs onto her house when it is swept downriver
during a flood. (1.Floods-Fiction  2.Courage-Fiction)
I.Devlin, Harry joint author. II.Title
PZ7D49875Han (E) 79-19400

ISBN 0-9669196-0-2

Dedicated to

Our Grandson Saxon

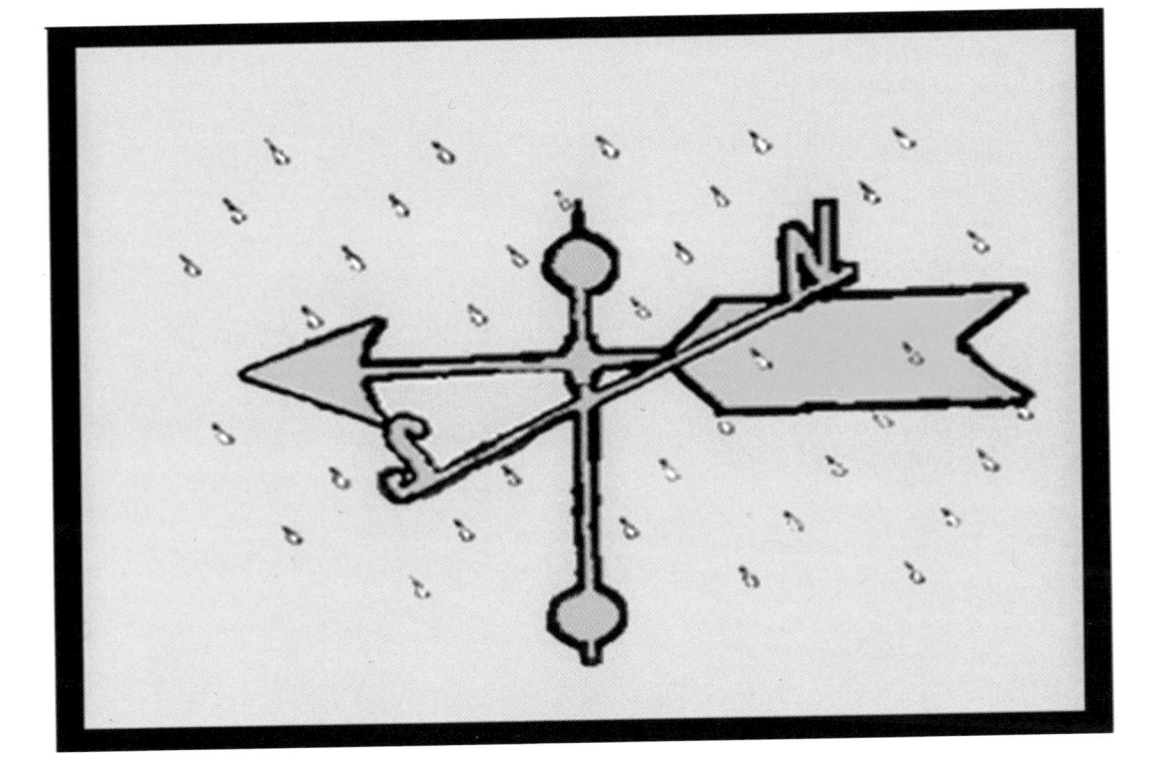

Presented to

_____

# Preface

Writing and illustrating our 32 children's books have given us great pleasure. We are happy to present the story of

"Hang  On , Hester !"
A Story of Courage and the Power of Example

The original edition, published in 1980 used the Offset Printing Process. Creating this new edition required reworking the illustrations. We are most grateful to–

Dorothy  C.  Nelson

for the countless hours of graphic work that have made this edition possible.

It is our wish that this book find its way into the homes and lives of children everywhere, those who are well and especially those who are ill.

May the story and example of Hester be an inspiration and example to them and their parents as well.

*Wende  and  Harry  Devlin*

Away up the river at
Hester's house it was raining.
While her mother and father
were doing important things,
Hester and Red Moose were left
in charge of the little farmhouse.
*Splash! Splash!! Splash!!!*
The rain fell on the roof.

Hester watched the rising river from
the kitchen window. She felt quite alone
and left out of things.

"I'd like to do important things too!
I'd like to see the world and have the
world see me," she said to Red Moose.

Then Hester dreamed aloud:

"Shall I be a doctor and save lives or an artist and paint pictures? What do you think, Red Moose?"

Red Moose thumped his tail. Whatever Hester decided to do would be all right with him. He thought everything about Hester was absolutely wonderful.

And outside it rained harder.

*Splash!  Splash!!  Splash!!!*

It rained and splashed and splashed and rained. Now the water rose higher and higher. Soon the river overflowed and reached out, covering roads and fields.

Hester opened the front door. The noise of the river was terribly close and Hester saw a world of water all around.

"The little dam above the farm must have broken," she said to Red Moose.

Now rushing, swirling waters rose to the doorstep. "Upstairs, Red Moose!" Hester shouted, as she grabbed her rubbers and her red raincoat. And up they ran, up the stairs to the second floor and up a steep staircase to the attic.

As the water rose higher Hester put
on her coat and rubbers. She and Red
Moose climbed into the cupola at the very
top of the house–and just in time!

The house creaked!

The house rocked!

Now there was a sound of wood leaving
stone and Hester's house began to move.
Soon it was floating, bobbing and swaying
down the green river.

Hester pushed the slats out of
the cupola. She climbed carefully up
to the old weather vane and hung on.

And down the river they bobbed–
a house, a red dog and a small girl.

Neighbors saw them floating by and shouted, "Hang on, Hester!" Hester hung on. She hung on past the farms. She hung on through the village.

All the way down the river, she hung on. "Hang on, Hester!" shouted people along the river bank.

Hester hung on. Someone phoned
to the city ahead and told the people
to watch out for a brave girl and a dog
floating down the river on a house.

By now, everyone knew about Hester
hanging on. She passed a factory.

"Hang on, Hester!" the workers
shouted. Hester hung on.

She sailed by the firehouse.

The firemen waved and cheered.

"Hang on, Hester!"

Hester's house floated to the city
where a bridge crossed the river.

People were crowded on the bridge
to help Hester.

The mayor was there
and so was the governor.
There were cameras and
excited newspapermen.

A policeman in blue and gold stepped
to the edge of the bridge. Keeping an
eye on Hester, he lowered a life preserver.
"Catch it, Hester", he shouted.

The moment had come.
Hester reached.  Hurrah! Hester caught
the swinging target.

Hester reached for Red Moose, but the dog leapt into the water. Moose was a fine swimmer and he headed towards shore.

Hester hung on tightly. And the house swept away below. "What a brave girl!" said the mayor, as he helped her up and over.

"Brave Hester!" the people cheered.

"Our Hester", said her parents,
as they hugged her close.
Red Moose barked on shore.
Hester and Moose were safe.

By morning the whole world
was talking about Hester.

A few days later, the flood went down
and Hester's house was hauled back
on a big tow truck.

The mailman was right behind the truck
with a sackful of mail for Hester.

"Why, you are famous Hester,"
said her mother, holding up a handful
of letters.

Hester and Red Moose sat in the sun
while Hester read the letters out loud.
The first one was from a painter who
had slipped from his ladder. "I held on
to the eaves until help came," he wrote.
"If you could, so could I"

Far over the sea, a mountain climber fell and rolled to the cliff's edge. His friends found him later, hanging on a branch.

"Little Hester hung on," he whispered. "That gave me courage."

Over in Sayertown, a farmer's wife had been chased up an apple tree by a spotted cow.

"I thought of you, Hester, and I hung on," She had written.

Far off in Africa, a schoolboy
chased by ten elephants, climbed
high on a vine and hung on. His arms
were tired, but he thought of Hester.

The elephants thundered by below
and he slipped down the vine safely.

Hester was pleased with the letters.

Red Moose looked pleased too.

"Well," said Hester to Red Moose,
"today if somebody asked me
how to see the world and have
the world see them,

I'd say, 'Just hang on!'
No matter what happens.
Hang On!"

Red Moose thumped his tail.
He thought everything Hester said
was simply wonderful.

# A Meland Foundation Edition

The Foundation derives its name from a Place, a Spirit, and a Family.

*The Place:* **Meland, Norway — hardly a village, but a cluster of houses and small farms in picturesque Southern Norway.**

*A Spirit:* **a love of home and family; courage and hope; and a deep religious faith that sustained them on a difficult journey.**

*A Family:* **led by Martin Meland Nelson, father of The Foundation Founder and President.**

## The Mission of The Foundation is twofold.

*To provide* **accurate information on Medicine and Health, without charge and without advertising, to enable each of us to make wise decisions concerning our health and well being.**

*To distribute* **and produce literature that will build hope and courage, to enable each of us to acheive our highest potential, and bring honor to Family, God, and Country.**

The stability, direction, and strength of The Foundation is derived from its traditions, its mission, and its associations.

# The Board of Trustees

# The Meland Foundation
# Network For Medical and Health Information
### Box 234 Harrington Park, NJ 07640

www.melandfoundation.org
e-mail melandfoundation@usa.net

### Englewood Hospital and Medical Center
### 201-894-3145
### Fax: 201-541-3446

### Closter Public Library
### 201-768-4100
### Fax: 201-768-2622

# Wende and Harry Devlin

Are outstanding and well known artists and writers.

They have written and illustrated over 32 children's books,

including

*The Old Black Witch and The Cranberry Series*

Harry's prize-winning *Portraits of American Architecture* from 1830 to 1920 includes many of his magnificent paintings. Wende's poetry series *Beat Poems of a Beat Mother* published by *Good Housekeeping* has received many accolades.

Wende and Harry shared the <u>Arent's Medal</u>, the highest alumni award from Syracuse University. Both are members of <u>The Literary Hall of Fame</u> and have received many other honors and awards.

Wende and Harry have seven children and eighteen grand-children. They have a charming home with a separate studio in Mountainside, New Jersey.

# *Notes*